Praise for Matt Haig and Chris Mould

'Absolutely brilliant'
CBBC

'Amazing'
Blue Peter

'Lovely, warm, enveloping'
Guardian

'Full of heart and humour'
Daily Express

'Charming'
Mail on Sunday

Also by Matt Haig

THE TRUTH PIXIE

MATT HAIG

with illustrations by
CHRIS MOULD

CANONGATE

First published in Great Britain in 2018
by Canongate Books Ltd,
14 High Street, Edinburgh EH1 1TE

canongate.co.uk

6

Copyright © 2018, Matt Haig
Illustrations copyright © 2018, Chris Mould

The moral right of the author has been asserted

British Library Cataloguing-in-Publication Data
A catalogue record for this book is available on
request from the British Library

ISBN 978 1 78689 432 8

Typeset by Canongate Books Ltd

Printed and bound in Great Britain
by Clays Ltd, Elcograf S.p.A.

To Pearl and Lucas

In a land two thousand miles from here,
Is a place where snow falls all the year.
There you find trolls and goblins and elves,
And talking rabbits, rather pleased with themselves.

Other odd creatures live there as well,
Like this Truth Pixie, whose tale I shall tell.

Truth Pixie's sad, as she's not like the others,
She's not like her nineteen sisters or thirty-eight brothers.

She's not like her brother Brian who dances and sings,
She's not like her sister Sylva with bright shiny wings.

She can't tell stories, she can't sing songs,
She can't do magic, she can't right wrongs.
In fact, for a pixie, she is quite peculiar,
And the reason for that is her great-aunt Julia.

When she was young, Aunt J cast a spell,
She said, 'From this day on, the truth you shall tell.'
To be the Truth Pixie, that is her curse,
She must tell the truth, for better or worse.
Imagine!

Wherever she is, whatever the day,
She only has one kind of thing to say.

Just as cats go

And cows go

moo

The Truth Pixie can only
Say things that are **true**.

It's good to never tell a lie,

That's what people always say,

But they've probably never met the Truth Pixie,

On a cold Midwinter's day.

If she'd done something wrong, she'd have to confess,

And if you looked scruffy she'd say,

What a mess!

So, the pixie stays alone in her little yellow house,
With no friends, except for a strange brown mouse.
The mouse is called Maarta and lives in her hair.
Yes, that's right. Her hair, **look**, the mouse is there!

The pixie looks at her empty shelves,
'We must go to town to feed ourselves.'
The Truth Pixie sighs
As she puts on a shoe,

She's ever so lonely,
But what can she do?

To make good friends, it shouldn't be hard.
Invite them to dinner, send them a card,

Sing them a song, or have a party,
Be super kind and dress really smartly.

Well, poor TP – she's tried this and more,
But now look – she's scared to leave her own door.
No matter the card, no matter the song,
Something always – ALWAYS – goes wrong.

Like the time she made dinner for an elf named Tinky,
And said that her breath was far too stinky.
Or when she had a party for her sister Amelie,
And sang 'Happy Birthday' in front of her family.

So her family got cross,
And never came back.
And where there were friends,
There was now a big lack.

So the Truth Pixie decided
(Along with her mouse),
To give up on friends,
And stay sad in her house.

'Truth shouldn't hurt people,
Truth shouldn't surprise,
But, oh Maarta, it does!
I so wish I'd tell lies.
When I go out, I hope to see
Absolutely no one, except you and me.'

The Truth Pixie looks in the mirror
And tells herself, 'Don't cry.'
Even as she wipes
A lonely tear from her eye.

And so she is off,
Walking fast into town,
Trying to look unfriendly,
And keep her head down.

24

But OH NO!

What's this over here?

An elf waving,

And grinning ear to ear.

The Truth Pixie tries to hide
Inside a big bush,
And says to her mouse,
'Please, Maarta! Shush!'
But it's too late, she knows it's true,
'Cos the elf is saying, 'How do you do?'

Of course, most people would say,
'I'm fine, have a nice day!'
And then they'd happily be on their way.
But the Truth Pixie can't just be polite;
This pixie tells the truth if it takes until night.

So she breathes deep, and closes her eyes . . .
'Well, I'm feeling dreadful, and that's no lie.
And, now that you ask, if you really must know,
When I left the house, I stubbed my big toe.
But that's not the trouble, not really, no.

The trouble is

these truths just won't let go!

Every elf or pixie who asks me a question,
Gets a horrible truth I can't help but mention.
So, I'm stressed in bed and stressed on the loo,
And the mouse in my hair has just done a poo.'

'Okay. Right,' says the elf, backing away.
'Is that the time? . . . Maybe another day!'

Our pixie – poor pixie – waves bye and feels sad.

'I reply to their questions, but they just think I'm mad.

I don't know how to stop doing what I do,

Without answering questions with things that are true.'

The Truth Pixie carries on with her walking,
And hopes she won't have to do any more talking.
'I wish there was someone who could handle the truth.
But there isn't. And my lonely heart is the proof.'

As she reaches town, the road becomes busy,
The Truth Pixie's fear of questions is making her dizzy.

'Do you like my hair?' another elf enquires.

'Hmm. It looks like a thousand ugly wires.'

'What about my clothes? I got them from this
    great place.'

'Well, to be fair, they're better than your face.'

The elf is angry and goes bright red.

Along comes a rabbit, fluffy and brown,
Wondering about the Truth Pixie's frown.

The Truth Pixie groans and speaks without blinking:
'I'm thinking that rabbits are the oddest things ever,
Floppy-eared weirdos who aren't very clever.

I'm thinking, I wish they didn't go shopping,
When they can't even walk, and insist upon hopping,

And I keep on stepping in their gross round droppings –
I'm sorry for the truth but it's just not stopping . . .'

The Truth Pixie bites her own hand
And runs down the street,
Until she looks up,
And sees two massive feet.

Too late!

Crash! And bump!

She bangs into a foot

And a big warty lump!

The foot is so huge and knobbly and wide,
The pixie feels fear all through her insides.
'I'm so sorry! I didn't see where I was going!
But hey, look at that, I think it's stopped snowing!'

41

35ft

The Truth Pixie stares up and up to the sky.
Her heart beats fast and there's no wondering why –
The person she's met is no person at all
But a troll who's way over thirty feet tall.

20ft

10ft

She knows of the troll.
She's seen him before.
He likes to start fights and
Is best to ignore.

He picks up the pixie to get a close look.
The Truth Pixie read about this in a book.
She's pulled high in the sky, trapped in his fist.
'Let me go! To my house, there, through the mist!'

Your new house be soon in my big
   greedy tum!'
'Wait! Wait!' TP squeaks. 'Don't be so hasty!
I may look sweet, but I'm bony not tasty.'
'**Hmm,**' grumbles the troll. '**Then please
   tell me,**
**What can you do to stay out
   of my belly?**'

The Truth Pixie gulps,
The Truth Pixie is scared.
The Truth Pixie knows
that the truth can't be shared.

She tries to think, as the troll's face comes near,
But it's hard to think with a brain full of fear.

'Maybe,' the troll says, 'you is not my food,
Tell me a story, but make it good!
Come on. Speak up. What's the matter
with you?'

The Truth Pixie sighs. 'It has to be true.'

He holds the poor creature, and squeezes her tight.
'Oh, this be perfect! This be so right!
You see, I scare every creature
    and every bird,
So the truth be something
    I never 'ave heard!'

'But,' says the pixie, in a rather quick blurt,
'You should know that the truth can sometimes hurt.'

'Well, listen now, Pixie, and listen hard!
Look at my arms! Look how I be scarred!
I be tough as rock and as strong as stone,
I've no fear in my blood and none in my bone.

I eat monsters for breakfast and beasts for my tea!
There's nothing that scares me, don't you see?
The truth won't hurt. I'm too tough for that.
I'm no big soft fluffy scaredy cat.'

'Cat?'

Says the mouse in the Truth Pixie's hair.
And she looks for a cat but no cat is there.

The troll keeps talking, with breath that does stink,

'Tell me, Truth Pixie, WHADDYA FINK?'

The Truth Pixie tries to hold her mouth closed,
She covers her lips and breathes out of her nose.
But the truth is strong,
The truth can't be planned.
And so the truth comes fast,
And down goes her hand.

'What do I think? . . . I have nothing to say.'

Agh!

Oh no!

The words are
on their way!

'I think you are **lumpy** and **warty** and **stupid**,

I think you are **smelly** and **ugly** and **putrid**,

I think you are **dumb** and not in a fun way,

If you were a plane you'd get **stuck on the runway**!

I think your teeth are **yellow** and **brown**,

I think you should be careful when you come to town.

Your feet are too **stompy** and you make people **shake**,

You are a **giant horrendous walking earthquake**.

You eat people who really shouldn't be eaten,
And once crushed a whole town in a land called Sweden.
You're a nasty troll who smells like wee . . .
And now,
I suppose,
You're still going

     to

          eat

               me.'

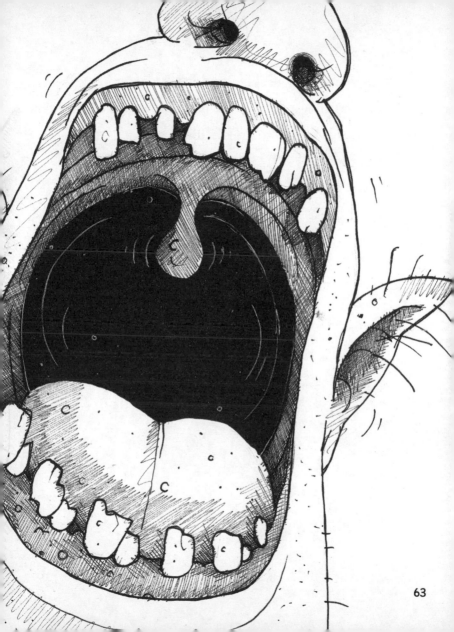

The Truth Pixie closes her eyes

The troll opens wide and is ready to munch . . .

'I be mad!
  And I be cross!
I need to show
    Who be the boss!

I should eat you up,
    I really should!
But you'll taste like the truth
    And that be no good.'

So, the giant troll gets ready to throw . . .

And into the air the pixie does go!

She flies over fields and over mountains,
She flies over palaces and pretty fountains.

She flies over horses eating hay.
One looks up at the sky and shouts, 'Neigh!'

She spins and twists and rolls through the air,

As Maarta grips on to her fast-blowing hair.

She's thrown so far by that troll who is stinky,
That she arrives in a town now known as Helsinki.

She drops through a window on the edge of town,
And sees a human in a dressing gown.
The girl on the bed hugs a pillow patterned with foxes,
She sits and cries in a room full of boxes.

'Who are you?' says the girl. 'And what are you doing?'
The Truth Pixie sighs. Is more trouble brewing?
'I'm the Truth Pixie and I was hoping you'd ignore me.
Because I can't sing songs and I can't tell a story.
Just as cats go miaow and cows go moo,
The Truth Pixie can only say things that are true.

Far away is the home where I belong,
I got thrown by a troll who found the truth too strong.
I've upset two elves and a rabbit who hops,
I hate this truth, it just never stops.
I'm the most miserable thing you ever did see,
I upset people just by being me.'

The girl smiles softly. 'I know the feeling!'
She looks sadly up to the ceiling.
'My name is Aada. It has three As.
We're moving house in just two days.'

The Truth Pixie feels bad. She can see the girl's truth.
This is nearly her last night under this roof.
There are other things, too, that the pixie can see:
Aada's hundred worries, about what will be.

'You are the Truth Pixie! Tell me how this ends.
Can I stay in this town, with all my friends?
Will my father keep his job? Will my gran get better?
Was the doctor lying, in his scary letter?'

The Truth Pixie hears this and knows she can't leave.

She must answer with truth, but make her believe.

'Listen, Aada, I know it's a blow,

The answer to your questions,' she says, 'is no.'

Aada goes pale, Aada can't speak.

Aada feels scared and a little bit weak.

The Truth Pixie knows she's made this day worse.

She HATES the truth, She HATES her curse.

She watches Aada get sadder and sadder,
As if stuck down a hole without a ladder.
Then the pixie wonders if she can find
A ladder of words, for Aada to climb.

'Listen, Aada, I have something to say.
The truth can be hard, that is its way.
You will have to move house, as your dad has no money,
You will have to lose friends, and that isn't funny.

There will be people you love,
Who can't stay for ever,
And there will be things you can't fix,
Although you are clever.

But listen hard, and listen good.

Life might not go as it should,

But you are young and your life will be magic,

It will be happy and funny and sometimes tragic.

Don't forget who you are. You are a fighter.

As the dark in the sky makes the stars shine brighter,

You will find the bad stuff has good bits too.

The bad days are the days that make you *you*.

You can't always see goodness, but it's always there,
Just like the mouse who hides in my hair.

If everything was perfect, every single day,
You'd never know the good from the just-about-okay.
The truth is, your future will often be great,
It's bad now you're seven, but wait till you're eight.

You will make new friends, as good as the old,
Friends who'll warm your heart against the cold.
The house you move to will be smaller than here,
But you'll be so happy there, this time next year.

The best things in life are yet to come,

You'll read great books and you'll have great fun.

You'll have a pet cat you'll name after your gran . . .'

'Cat?' worries Maarta. 'It's time I ran!'

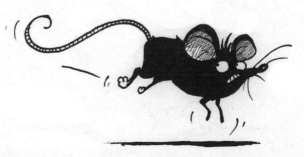

The rest of your life is full of good stuff,
You'll travel the seas, both calm and rough.
It's up to you, wherever you go,
The sun of the desert, the cold of the snow.

You'll eat ice cream tasting of strawberry and rose,
You'll feel happiness from your head to your toes.
You'll love your pet cat, and she'll enjoy a cuddle,
And you'll dance and sing and splash in a puddle!
You'll have fun at Christmas, and Easter too,
In summer you'll sometimes go to the zoo.

You'll laugh at bad jokes, and fall off a chair,
Feel the sun on your face and the wind in your hair.
You see, your life is like a voice,
How you use it, is really your choice.
You can live life as a mumble, or sing it clear,
But it will often be special, you'll be glad to hear.

You'll have so many moments – whole years –
    full of fun,
That will be there just waiting once these sad
    days are done.
Sure, life isn't always one big smile,
But things turn out fine, when you wait a while.

97

Yes, the night has dark bits, but it has stars too,

And you'll feel when they shine,

That they shine just for you.

You will step outside, and see from the park

That the light is brighter

When it's next to the dark.

You will have so many great times ahead,
And soft happy dreams from inside your bed.
The future is changing, a life is a mix,
A life's made of hope like a house is of bricks.
And tonight, right now, you feel very sad,
But the rest of your life won't be so bad.'

Aada listened and Aada heard,
Aada hung on every word.
Aada knows the pixie is right,
The present is dark but the future is bright.
'Thank you, Truth Pixie, you have made things clear;
I will cry today but I won't cry all year.
It's all a bit weird, and a little bit mad,

But you'll never know happy unless you know Sad.

The Truth Pixie starts to feel a bit pleased.
Aada gives Maarta some very fine cheese.
The pixie sighs. 'I guess I should go.'

The girl thinks hard and then says,

'The Far North,' says the pixie, 'is where I belong.'
But even as she says it she feels it is wrong.

Aada stands up and looks very serious,
'Listen,' she says, 'it's not so mysterious.
You've just said that life is what we choose,
If you stay with me you've nothing to lose.'

The Truth Pixie thinks.

The Truth Pixie ponders.

The
Truth Pixie
Wonders.

'With you? Are you sure? But what about your dad?'

'Dad talks about pixies when he thinks I am sad.

He won't mind. He likes my friends.'

'Really?' says the pixie. And her heart starts to mend.

'But what about Maarta, when you get your new cat?'
'Hmm. Yes. We'll need to think about that!
Maybe I'll get a dog instead.
The future keeps changing, that's what you said.'

The Truth Pixie
Smiles
from ear to ear,

Her first actual
smile
in over a year.

Thank you,
Aada.
Thanks for being you.
Thanks
for making
me
glad to be
true

And Aada smiles back, and looks out at the sky.

The pixie is proud that she never did lie.

Aada's father walks in and sees the creature there,

With its big bright eyes, and a mouse in its hair.

Then he sees something stranger,

That he couldn't replace,

A smile on his daughter's once sad face.

'Oh Pixie,' he says. 'Thank you a lot!
Aada wanted a smile and now that's what she's got.
You must stay with us, if you've no better plan.
Join us for supper, there's soup in the pan!'

'Oh, thank you,' says TP, 'you're so very kind!
Can my mouse join us too, if you really don't mind?'
Aada laughs, and her father laughs too,
And the Truth Pixie laughs,
And the laugh feels new.

The pixie still lives there to this day.
Her truth no longer needs to hide away.
That's the power of a loving friend.

And here's the part
where we say . . .

As well as being a number one bestselling writer for adults, **Matt Haig** has won the Blue Peter Book Award, the Smarties Book Prize and been shortlisted three times for the Carnegie Medal for his stories for children and young adults.

Chris Mould went to art school at the age of sixteen. He has won the Nottingham Children's Book Award and been commended by the Sheffield Children's Book Award. He loves his work and likes to write and draw the kind of books that he would have liked to have had on his shelf as a boy. He is married with two children and lives in Yorkshire.

Cover design by Rafaela Romaya
Cover illustration © Chris Mould
Author photograph © Jonny Ring